Jazeera
in the Sun

Also by Lisa Bruce

Jazeera's Journey
Nani's Holiday

Banana Books
Sister of the Bride

Lisa Bruce

Jazeera in the Sun

Illustrated by Paul Howard

MAMMOTH

To my mother-in-law
for all her help and support

First published in Great Britain 1995
by Methuen Children's Books Ltd
Published 1996 by Mammoth
an imprint of Reed International Books Ltd,
Michelin House, 81 Fulham Road, London SW3 6RB
and Auckland, Melbourne, Singapore and Toronto

Text Copyright © 1995 Lisa Bruce
Illustrations Copyright © 1995 Paul Howard

The right of Lisa Bruce to be identified as author of this
work has been asserted by her in accordance with
the Copyright, Designs and Patents Act 1988

ISBN 0 7497 1988 5

A CIP catalogue record for this book
is available at the British Library

Printed in Great Britain
by Clays Ltd, St Ives plc

Contents

1. Here Comes the Sun

Dear Diary,

We are off at last. I hope that I have remembered to pack everything. Omar wanted to bring his Superman jumper and he kicked up a real fuss when Mummy wouldn't let him. She said that it will be much too hot for jumpers in India. It's funny, but I don't remember it being very hot, just nice. I told Mummy that if it was going to be so hot then I would need a new pair of sandals but she wouldn't buy me any. She said that we can buy things like that cheaper once we get there.

I can't wait to arrive. We've got nine hours in this aeroplane before we get there, though. I have brought some books to read and Omar is busy doing some colouring. Still, we can't do that for another nine hours. And what about Azra? Now that she is crawling, she is not going to want to sit still for all that time.

I'll have to stop, now. Something smells nice and I can see the stewardess coming this way with a big trolley.

I've just had a meal and I must write this down before we land, otherwise I will forget. Omar and I were allowed to visit the cockpit. Silly Omar called it the cockroach! It was fascinating. Four men sat surrounded by gleaming panels of instruments. They looked very important. Mind you, Daddy said afterwards that he was a little bit worried that they had all been reading newspapers when we went in! Omar asked lots of questions and the pilot was very nice to him. They even showed us how to tell which country we were flying over. Now all Omar talks about is being

a pilot when he grows up!

After that we all watched a video and fell asleep before we were given another meal. We are coming into Delhi now, and my ears are hurting as we go down. Somehow the time has passed really quickly. I'm not tired. I shall want to go to sleep in the middle of the afternoon. Right now, though, I'm wide awake and looking forward to seeing Nani.

'Aieee . . . Jazeera! How are you, *beyti*?'

The cry reached Jazeera's ears the moment that she passed through the large double doors and out into the Delhi sunshine. For an instant Jazeera recoiled. The sunshine dropped itself over her and smothered her. She felt as though she had smacked into a wall of heat.

Jazeera didn't have time to recover before a slight figure threw her arms around Jazeera's shoulders and kissed her. The heat and Nani's weight was too much for Jazeera – she nearly staggered.

'Nani!' she cried as she realised who it was.

'Here, Jazeera, let me take that from you.'

It was Uncle Salim. Jazeera allowed the strap to be slipped from her shoulder and then threw her arms around her grandmother.

'Nani, look, I'm nearly as tall as you, now!'

'Not quite, little one,' laughed Nani.

'Now, where's everyone else?'

'They're right behind, Nani. I didn't want to wait so . . .'

'Omar!' cried Nani. 'Be careful. You musn't push the trolley into your sister like that. Come here and give your old Nani a kiss.'

Omar did as he was told while Jazeera rubbed her sore leg, angrily. The metal edges of the suitcase had scratched her bare skin. Her parents arrived, scolding Omar for running away with the trolley and then greeted Nani and Uncle with delight.

'Come along, everyone,' called Uncle Salim in his rich, deep voice. 'The car is over here!'

As they threaded their way across the roughly tarmacked car park, the family acquired quite a crowd of curious onlookers. Most of them were offering to carry the suitcases in return for a small tip but some were beggars.

Jazeera had forgotten about the beggars. One of the girls looked about the same age as herself except her clothes were in tatters and covered in layers of grime. On her hip she supported a straggly infant, dressed only in a dirty grey vest, who stared at Jazeera with large pleading eyes. The girl didn't speak, she simply looked hungrily at Jazeera's neat pink satin dress, her white ankle socks and her sturdy black school shoes.

Jazeera felt awkward under the constant staring.

'She must think that I am rich,' Jazeera whispered to Nani.

'Compared to her, you are,' Nani answered as she watched the men load the heavy suitcases into the boot of the waiting car.

The girl's eyes never left Jazeera.

Jazeera thought back to all the times that she had pestered her mother to buy her things from the High Street, because Moni or one of her other friends had them. She had forgotten what it was like to live among people who had nothing. Jazeera felt uncomfortable. The sun pressed constantly on her body, bringing out prickles of sweat, and still the girl's eyes never left her.

The bags were squashed into position and the family settled themselves into the car.

'You can fit in here, Jazeera,' called her uncle.

But Jazeera didn't move. She was held captive by the girl's stare. Nani moved over and slipped a folded note into the girl's free hand. Instantly the spell was broken. The girl turned and fled with surprising speed considering the weight of the heat and the child.

'What did you give her, Nani?'

'Five rupees, I think that is ten pence in your money. That will feed her for today at least.'

Jazeera smiled sadly as she climbed into the hot, crowded car. What would her life be like if she had to survive from begging? she thought.

On the way to Nani's house they passed many beggars, some with arms or legs missing and all looking hungry. But somehow Jazeera couldn't get the picture of the little girl out of her mind. She hoped that she had bought something nice to eat and that she wasn't hungry any more.

Dear Diary,

How different everything is here, how different and yet the same. I can't explain it, it's like walking into a living dream – Nani's house, my old room, the piano, they are all just how I remember them. But yet they are not exactly the same. In the garden the trees are much smaller than I remember them. They must have shrunk since we left, or perhaps I have grown. I remember the verandah as being so high above the

lawn but actually it is only three steps! I could jump over all of them now if I wanted to. If it wasn't too hot to jump, that is.

I certainly don't remember this heat. All my clothes feel sticky and uncomfortable. I keep going into the bathroom to splash cold water on my face, then Aunty told me that they have water restrictions at the moment so I have to be careful how much I use. It is very important that we don't leave the taps running because once the tank's empty, that's it – no more water until the next morning. I'll have to keep an eye on Omar, he is always playing with water!

Ayisha is coming around to see us tomorrow. She is at school at the moment. I hope that she hasn't changed too much. I'd better finish now, Mummy is calling me to have a drink. I hope that they've got Thums Up. That's one thing that I really have missed.

2. Busy Bazaar

With curtains drawn against the fierce midday sun Jazeera and her family sat beneath the whirring fans in the living room. Azra, clothed in just her nappy, wobbled precariously from one adoring adult to the next. Jazeera and Omar sat slowly sipping the deliciously cool fizzy drinks, allowing the chill of the bottle to spread through their baking palms. Between them, Nani sat with her cup of tea.

Beside them was the piano where Jazeera had first acquired her love of music. On top of the piano, in pride of place, stood the silver photo frame that Jazeera had given Nani at her surprise seventy-fifth birthday party. Inside was a faded photograph of a handsome smiling man: Jazeera's Nana. Jazeera had bought the silver frame from Bentley's, a large department store in her High Street and it reminded her sharply of England.

Jazeera couldn't get over how much smaller everything was, the room, the piano, even Nani. The figure beside her seemed to have shrunk since their last meeting.

'Tell me about school,' Nani said. 'How are Amy and Moni?'

'Oh, they're fine. Amy won the Interschools Running Trophy this year. Mrs Levin presented the trophy to her in assembly but she tripped over as she went up to the stage and she knocked one of her front teeth out. There was blood everywhere and now Amy has got to have a false tooth made. Mrs Levin says that it was her own fault for going so fast. I think that she was just showing off because she had won a running trophy.

'Yes and I got splattered with some of the blood,' said Omar proudly. 'Because I was sitting in the front row.'

'Did you?' said Nani.

'Yes AND our class went to visit a farm AND I saw some pigs and some sheep AND I touched a cow, it was very warm . . .'

'Well, there are lots of cows for you to see here, Omar,' Nani laughed. 'They walk wherever they like in the streets, but I shouldn't go touching them if I were you.'

'I won't, Nani . . . What's that?'

'What's what?'

'That noise, what is it?'

'Oh, that's Uncle, I expect that he's going down to the shop.'

'But, Nani, look . . . He's got a scooter.'

With that, Omar fled through the screened door, out into the glare of the garden. Uncle saw him coming and slowed his journey down the driveway, stopping the bright yellow scooter just

short of the gates.

Omar gazed at the machine in awe.

'Would you like a ride?' Uncle asked, mischievously.

Omar didn't wait to be asked twice, he ran up to the scooter and scrambled up on to the wide leather seat.

'Hold your horses,' said Uncle. 'Why don't you go and ask Jazeera if she would like to come, too.'

In a trice Omar was off the scooter and running back into the house. He skidded to a stop in front of his sister and grabbed her arm.

'Come on, come on,' he yelled.

Jazeera was in the middle of describing her class visit to a glass-making factory and she pulled her arm away from Omar, angrily. 'What do you want?'

All Omar could say in his excitement was, 'Come on, come on,' as he tugged even harder at Jazeera's arm, almost pulling her out of the chair.

'Go and see what he wants,' suggested Nani. 'You can finish telling me about the factory later.'

So Jazeera got up and followed a dancing Omar outside. As she passed the window one of the curtains flapped lazily in the gentle breeze of the fan and Jazeera saw Nani sitting in the chair with her head back and her eyes closed.

'Oh, there you are, Jazeera,' called Uncle. 'Hop on.'

Before she knew what was happening Jazeera had been helped up on to the back seat and shown where to put her feet. Uncle settled himself in front of her and Omar stood between his arms on the footplate.

The gates were opened and the scooter revved into life.

At first Jazeera clung on to her uncle, afraid that she would fall off, but the scooter didn't go very fast and Jazeera soon relaxed. She began to enjoy the sensation of the hot air brushing its fingers through her loose hair. At least it was no longer stuffy. She closed her eyes and soaked up the warmth all around her.

Suddenly the bike jumped. Jazeera was thrown upwards, violently, and then crashed back into her seat with a mighty force. Her eyes pounced open in panic and her arms automatically gripped the soft flesh of her uncle's middle.

'What was that?'

'It's only a speedbreaker,' Uncle called, his voice faint in the rushing wind.

Jazeera looked back and saw a raised hump of concrete running across the width of the road.

'They are to stop the traffic from going too fast,' Uncle explained.

Jazeera decided that if the ride was going to be as bumpy as that then she'd better keep her eyes open from now on.

When they reached Uncle's shop in the busy shopping district, Omar's face was shining with glee.

'I want a motorbike,' he breathed with determination as he stepped off the purring machine.

'You'll have to ask Mummy about that,' Jazeera said sceptically. 'They are very expensive.'

'I'll save up all my pocket money and buy my own, so there.'

'The motorbikes at home go much faster than these and they are much more dangerous. I don't think that she'll let you.'

Omar pouted his lips and flounced away from Jazeera. He never won when he argued with his sister. Just because she was older she thought that she knew everything. Well, he'd show her. Omar turned and followed his uncle into the little bangle shop.

Although Uncle's shop was small, every available space was used to display piles and piles of gleaming bangles. Stacked in packets of six or eight or ten, they filled the entire shop. Jazeera thought that she had never seen so many bangles altogether in one place. There were glass ones, plastic ones, glittery ones and jewelled ones.

Ibrahim, Uncle's helper, was serving two stout ladies. They wanted some bangles to match the colours in their new sarees and because the material was brightly patterned they couldn't decide which colour to match. In the end, Ibrahim persuaded them to have gold-coloured ones which went with all the colours. The two ladies departed satisfied.

Uncle needed to go to the bank, so

Jazeera and Omar sat themselves down on some unopened boxes containing yet more bangles. They were grateful when Ibrahim called to a young boy and sent him to buy cool drinks for them. Although they were inside the shop, there were no windows. They looked straight out on to the streets and the air

inside the shop was just as hot as outside.

As they waited for Uncle to return, Jazeera and Omar gazed at the passers-by on the busy street. People, bicycles, scooters and rickshaws surged up and down the narrow street in a brightly coloured river of traffic. All the time horns bipped, bells shrilled, and urgent voices shouted from one shop to another.

'Hey you, come here!'

BEEP.

'Move over, can't you.'

An ox-cart laden with sugar-cane sticks.

A bicycle.

A taxi.

People crossing the road.

BEEP BEEP.

'Move, come on!'

A bicycle swerving to miss an old lady.

Red sarees.

Yellow sarees.

28

Stray dogs scavenging in piles of litter.

HONK.

Sour smells.

'Careful!'

Snakes hypnotised by whining music .

BEEP BEEP BEEP.

A girl struggling, an enormous basket on her head.

Grain spilling out of sacks on to shop floors.

A scooter.

Two Scooters.

BIP BIP.

Orange Sarees.

Boys eating *chaat*.

A banana cart cutting across the road.

'Get out of the way.'

BEEP.

Another ox-cart.

A sugar-cane juicer whirring round and round.

Brightly coloured material flapping on poles outside a shop.

Dust everywhere.

BEEP BEEP.

Noise everywhere. All the time.

It was chaotic but at the same time fascinating. All these hundreds of people jammed together into a tiny space busily going about their own business.

Jazeera sipped her drink and turned her attention to a severe-looking woman who had just entered the shop. She was followed by three trailing daughters of various ages, all looking bored. The woman, who was obviously their mother, began choosing sets of bangles for each of her daughters, without once consulting them as to which colour they would prefer. The girls for their part stood in a disgruntled line and stared at Jazeera.

Jazeera felt uncomfortable and looked away. She didn't like being stared at and this was the second time in one day that it had happened. These girls, unlike the beggar, had no need of money. Jazeera turned to Ibrahim to avoid meeting the row of silent eyes. He was

arguing with their mother.

'But you must give me a better price than that.'

'Twenty rupees each.'

'But I'm buying six sets. I will give you a hundred rupees and no more.'

'Done!'

Ibrahim held out his hand for the crinkled note.

'You would not get bangles of this quality, for that price anywhere else, madam,' he smiled.

The woman snorted and ushered her reluctant brood back out into the busy street. Omar followed them and sat on the step outside.

Jazeera was confused. If the bangles were twenty rupees each, then six sets should have cost 120 rupees. That meant that Ibrahim had sold them too cheaply. He was cheating her uncle! Just then Uncle Salim returned. Before Jazeera had a chance to say anything, Ibrahim thrust the 100 rupee note into his hand.

'Six sets. I just sold six sets for a hundred rupees!' Ibrahim's eyes danced with glee.

'Very good,' Uncle congratulated him.

Jazeera couldn't stay quiet. 'Uncle,' she said softly. 'They should have been twenty rupees each.'

Uncle Salim looked at her worried face and crouched down beside her 'Let me explain,' he said. 'Shopping here is not like shopping in England, where everything has a fixed price on the label.

In India we argue about the price. The shopkeeper will start by saying a price much higher than he expects to get. Then the customer says a price much lower than he or she expects to pay. Slowly the shopkeeper lowers his price and the customer raises his until they both agree, somewhere in the middle.'

Jazeera frowned. 'That all sounds very complicated.'

'Yes,' laughed Uncle. 'But so much more fun than shopping in England. Ibrahim here is a very good salesman. One hundred rupees is much more than I would have sold the bangles for.' Uncle slapped Ibrahim playfully, on the back. 'I know that my shop is in good hands when I leave it with him. Now where is that brother of yours, Jazeera? It's time we were heading back.'

Together they left the shop and looked for Omar. They found him sitting outside, holding a fistful of money, surrounded by a gang of boys, one of whom was busy strapping Omar's

Mickey Mouse watch on to his thin wrist.

'Omar!' exclaimed Jazeera. 'What are you doing?'

Omar grinned as he stood up. 'I've sold my watch,' he announced, and he shoved the wodge of notes into his pocket.

'Whatever for?' Jazeera asked, shocked that Omar would do such a thing. But Omar wouldn't say. Instead he strode up to the scooter and stood in position ready to go.

Uncle winked at him. 'What an enterprising young man you are,' he laughed.

The journey back to Nani's house took much longer than Jazeera expected. For one thing they got caught in the mesh of workers returning home after their day's work. For another thing they encountered an enormous traffic jam.

Jazeera was tired. Her legs began to ache from their cramped position on the scooter, and once or twice Jazeera felt her eyelids drooping. She mustn't go to sleep now, she might lose her grip and fall off the scooter when Uncle made one of his sharp swoops.

At last, the scooter inched forward and when Uncle manoeuvred around an auto-rickshaw, Jazeera saw what the cause of the problem was.

A cow.

A scrawny cow with all its ribs poking out of its sides had decided to settle down for a sleep in the middle of a busy road junction. Everybody was edging their way carefully around it. Oblivious to all the confusion that it was causing, the cow slept on.

'Why don't the police move it away?' Jazeera asked.

'Why bother?' said Uncle patiently. 'Anyway it's a cow, they go where they like.' He steered the scooter around the slumbering animal and set off down the road at a more sensible speed.

It was very late when they reached the house. Omar was virtually asleep on his feet. Night had come down with its sudden cloak of darkness and the insects hummed busily to themselves as they went about their business in the cooler evening air.

Jazeera staggered off the scooter and into her father's arms. She was so tired that she drank only half of the glass of juice offered to her before she tumbled on to the hard mattress and was soon as soundly asleep as the cow had been.

3. Just a Servant

Dear Diary,

Ayisha came round today. It was just like old times. We went outside on the verandah, to play ball. She is the same old Ayisha, full of fun. She wants to have her hair cut but her mother won't let her. We talked and talked about everybody that I used to know. It's funny, but being with Ayisha I feel as though I have never been away.

Ayisha was very interested in Azra and wanted to play with her. The only trouble is that Azra has been off her food since we got here, and she is in a miserable mood. She will only go to Mummy or Nani. She won't even let me

*touch her, which is just as well because
I've got too many things to do . . .*

Jazeera pulled a bundle of papers out
from the bottom of her suitcase, where
they had lain, flat-packed for the
journey. They were letters from each of
her classmates to a boy called Anil Devi.

The previous year, Anil's father had
drowned in a flood that had washed
away his schoolhouse. Jazeera's class
had raised enough money, during their
charity book auction, to sponsor him
through school.

As well as the letters, Jazeera had a
box of books and toys from the class.
Anil had written to the class regularly
and sent photographs of himself and his
younger sister.

Jazeera looked down at the science set
and the Frisbee. She wouldn't mind
having those herself! But that was
selfish, Anil probably had no other toys.
Nani walked into the room, with arms
full of clean clothes.

'The *dhobi-wallah* has just dropped these off. I'll sort them out, then we can go.'

'Here, let me help,' offered Jazeera, taking the crisply folded sarees from the top of the pile and stacking them neatly in the cupboard.

'What is Anil like?' Jazeera asked, suddenly shy about meeting him.

Jazeera felt as though she knew him well, yet didn't know him.

'You'll find out, soon enough,' said Nani as she quickly wrapped a fresh white saree around herself.

Outside, Nani hailed an auto-rickshaw. Although Mrs Khan's house was not far away, the afternoon sun was hammering down mercilessly. It was far too hot to walk with the box of presents.

The battered, yellow and black vehicle crunched to a halt outside the gates. Jazeera and Nani climbed aboard. Even inside the shade of the auto-rickshaw the heat surrounded them uncomfortably. Nani began to fan herself.

'It really is unusually hot for this time of year,' she said breathlessly.

'The radio said this morning that we might be heading for a heat-wave,' said Jazeera.

'Oh dear, I do hope not, that would be too much.'

The auto-rickshaw pulled up outside

the large, wrought-iron gates of Mrs Khan's house. They were just the same as Jazeera remembered them. Some things didn't change at all.

Mrs Khan had changed, though, her hair had turned grey and wispy like winter mist. She rushed out of the house to greet them. Mrs Khan was an old friend of Nani's and she had also been Jazeera's teacher. Jazeera was surprised at how old she looked now, but she still had the same cheery smile, which Jazeera knew from experience could turn to steel in an instant.

'Good morning, miss,' Jazeera said politely.

'Now, now, there's no need for that. I'm retired now. You must call me Aunty.'

Mrs Khan smiled, ushering them through the door and into the comparatively cool living room.

'Anil will be here soon. He has just gone down to the shops. I suddenly realised that I was out of Thums Up. Oh dear, I do hope that he hurries, you must be ready for a drink.'

'It's all right, Aunty,' Jazeera couldn't imagine anyone having to hurry in that heat.

A moment later the gates clicked and Jazeera heard the squeak of a bicycle being pushed up the path. The door opened and there behind a large cardboard box of Thums Up was Anil. He was dressed in thin cotton trousers and a shirt that was too small for him. For a split second, he and Jazeera eyed each other, then Mrs Khan leapt up and directed Anil to the bottle opener.

Anil poured three large tumblers of the fizzy, brown drink and offered them to everybody. His large, black eyes were full of life and laughter but he performed his duties as a servant correctly before being invited to sit with the company.

'Come, Anil,' said Mrs Khan briskly. 'Come and see what Jazeera has brought you from England.'

Anil sat obediently on the floor at Jazeera's feet and stared at her, his eyes brimming with pleasure. Jazeera felt uncomfortable. She had forgotten that servants were not allowed to sit on the furniture. Jazeera picked up the sheaf of letters but she couldn't just pass them down. This was no way to get to know Anil, so with one swift movement Jazeera lowered herself to the hard tiles and sat beside him on the floor.

Anil's eyes widened in shock when he saw what Jazeera had done, then he grinned. 'Hello,' he said. 'I've wanted to meet you so much.'

'You have!' It was Jazeera's turn to be surprised.

'I've heard so much about you.'

'I've brought some letters,' Jazeera said lamely.

'Thank you.'

Anil started to read the top letter, one from Jazeera's teacher, Mr Foster. It told Anil all about the school sports day and how everyone was looking forward

to the summer holidays. Mr Foster was off to the Algarve for a painting holiday.

'I didn't know that!' exclaimed Jazeera, reading over Anil's shoulder.

All the letters said much the same thing: who had won which race and who was going where for the holidays, but Anil read each one carfeully then placed it beside him as though it were a treasured possession. He placed the last piece of paper beside him, neatly.

'I'm the only one in our whole school who gets so many letters,' he said proudly. 'Everyone thinks that I am very important.'

Anil's face grew serious for a moment. 'I do want to thank you for all the money that you have spent on me I . . . I don't know what to do in return.'

'Just do your best,' said Jazeera. 'That's what Nani always says to me.'

'But you have done so much . . .'

'Because we wanted to.'

'I just don't want to let you down.'

'Of course you won't let them down,'

interrupted Mrs Khan, gently putting her hand on Anil's shoulder. 'I've heard all about how hard you study every night, all on top of your job here. I hear things from your teachers, you know. They all speak very highly of you.'

A gleam appeared in Anil's eyes. 'Do they? Do they really?'

'I am sure that one day you will become a very famous doctor,' added Nani.

'Then when we are sick we will come to you, won't we, Nani?' said Jazeera.

Nani laughed. 'You can, Zeeraji. You can visit our Dr Anil, but I doubt if I will be around to see it.'

'Oh, don't be silly, Nani.'

'Now then, you two, why don't you open that box of goodies.' Mrs Khan nudged Anil. 'I'm dying to see what's inside.'

Anil did not need to be asked twice. He plunged his hands into the box and brought out delight after miraculous delight. For what seemed ordinary and everyday to Jazeera was a marvel to Anil's eyes. He ran his hands tenderly over an old Barbie doll, a present from Moni to Anil's sister. He sniffed the smooth bars of deeply scented soap, a gift to his mother, and his eyes nearly popped out of their sockets when he lifted out the science set. The class had clubbed together to buy it for him. It was the most fantastic thing Anil had ever seen.

'Close your mouth, Anil' Mrs Khan suggested. Anil didn't hear. He was

already concocting radio circuits with batteries and electro-magnets in his mind's eye. This was now the most precious thing that he owned. He couldn't wait to get started on it.

'An . . .il' His employer's voice gradually registered in his brain. 'Anil, perhaps you would like to take Jazeera out in the garden.'

'Of course, yes, I will . . . come on.'

Jazeera picked up the Frisbee. 'Would you like to play with this?'

Anil looked at the fluorescent yellow disc with curiosity. Another wonderful new thing. God was shining on him today. He couldn't believe his luck.

The afternoon sun was departing and with it, the intense heat of the day. Jazeera and Anil played Frisbee in the gathering shadows. She taught him how to flick his wrist to get the best curve from the disc.

Anil was good. He leapt and ran enthusiastically until, with one gigantic sweep, the Frisbee arced up and up and fell out of sight on Mrs Khan's roof.

'Oh dear,' gasped Jazeera.

Anil set off across the garden. 'Come on, the steps are this way.'

He led Jazeera around the back of the house and up the rough concrete steps which led to the spacious flat roof.

The roof, which hadn't been used since the last winter, was strewn with leaves and cobwebs. Jazeera started as a roof-coloured lizard, disturbed from its slumberings, darted over her foot.

'You can see a long way from up here,' said Anil, the Frisbee safely in his hand. He pointed at the darkening horizons. 'There's the mosque on that hill over there and, opposite, that's the village where I live.'

'But, Anil, that's miles away,' Jazeera said in astonishment. 'How do you get here?'

'I cycle. It's not far really.'

Jazeera thought about all the times that she had complained whenever she had to walk to the shops or to school. That was nothing compared to what skinny Anil did every day!

The cricket chorus struck up their peaceful chirping from the jasmine trees as the last rose-embers of the day sank behind the tall domed mosque.

'You have a hard life, Anil.'

'But, no. I am very happy. I am at school and I can help to support my mother by working here. And I have so many friends in England. What more could I want?'

'How about another game of Frisbee?'

Far in the distance huge black buzzards circled, swooping and diving over their prey, until finally they dropped out of sight.

4. What a Day!

Dear Diary,

Omar has been a pest recently. When Mummy asked him to put his clothes away, Omar said that he would do it for 150 rupees. Mummy just ignored him and told him to get on with it. To my surprise he folded all his clothes up extra neatly (which Mummy says now proves that he CAN do it!) and he put them all away.

When Uncle took him out for a ride on the famous scooter, Omar said that he would get down and open the gates for 100 rupees. Yesterday he said that he would fetch Nani's glasses' case for 200 rupees. Nobody paid any attention to him and we all thought that it was just one of Omar's silly games.

When nobody paid up Omar got really upset and he threw a terrible fit. He screamed so loudly that all the birds flew out of the bedroom in fright. Mummy had only just got Azra off to sleep and he disturbed her. Mummy was cross and shouted at Omar, which made him worse.

It was Uncle Salim who stepped in to rescue Omar. He said that although Omar had been very enterprising, he should really get people to agree his prices before doing any work. Uncle said that if Omar wanted to earn some money then he could help in the bangle shop. Of course Omar was delighted with that arrangement.

Nani is having a sleep, now. She has been doing that quite a lot, lately. Mummy says that it is the heat-wave. She says that it is getting everyone down.

Water is very short. We ran out

yesterday afternoon, it was awful. I can't wait for the rains to come, then Ayisha and I will dance outside in the garden like we used to. Uncle says that the rains are very late this year. I hope they come before we have to go home.

Tomorrow we are going to visit one of Daddy's cousins. I don't remember Daddy's cousins, I was very little the last time we met. Uncle is taking us in his car! The car is Uncle's pride and joy. He polishes it every weekend until you can see your face in the shiny black paintwork. I don't know why he bothers, it looks about a thousand years old and I have serious doubts about whether it will make it all the way . . .

Uncle's ancient black car creaked and groaned with the weight of all its passengers. It chugged painfully along the fiery roads until it reached the other side of town. With one final effort it lurched up the long driveway and spluttered to a thankful stop outside an imposing building.

Jazeera felt awed by the huge house before her. Squeezing out of the car, into the intense heat, the first thing that she saw was a very solemn-looking doorman dressed in a spotless white uniform topped by a splendid red turban. His nose lifted a fraction and his eyes never wavered, as he held open the ornate double doors to allow the family through.

Inside the hall the heat instantly shivered into air-conditioned chill. Fabulous rugs littered the cool, marble floor. Beautiful ornaments stood on gleaming table-tops beneath sparkling chandeliers.

'Don't touch anything, Omar!' hissed his mother.

But Omar was now just as shy as Jazeera. He held tightly on to Nani's hand while their father's cousin and his wife rushed forward to greet them all.

'Say hello to your aunty,' their mother insisted, pushing Omar and Jazeera

forward. Reluctantly they gave the dazzling lady a quick peck on the cheek.

The house breathed luxury from every corner and the children were on their best behaviour. Jazeera and Omar sat politely on either side of Nani and were careful not to touch anything. Biscuits and fresh lemonade were served by the haughty-looking man in the fancy turban, while their father's cousin talked in a loud voice about how successful his business had become.

Soon Azra woke up and gazed blankly at the chinking crystal chandelier above her. She was thirsty and began to whine for a drink. Aunty clapped her hands and another servant appeared with a frosted glass of lemon juice. Azra gulped it down, greedily.

'Come over here,' crooned Aunty. 'I do love babies. It's such a pity that I can't have any of my own.'

Jazeera's mother passed Azra over, hoping that the little girl wouldn't decide to have a yank at the expensive

jewellery, hanging enticingly around her aunty's slim neck. To her mother's relief Azra stayed still.

Very still.

'What a good girl you are,' smiled Aunty, bouncing Azra up and down on her silken knee. Azra's glazed eyes stared blankly at the pretty face and before anyone realised what was going to happen she opened her little mouth, and SPLURT!

She was sick.

Very sick.

All over Aunty's expensive, orange saree.

Their father's cousin stopped in mid-sentence. Jazeera's father and Uncle Salim both dropped their mouths open like two stunned goldfish. Nani, Jazeera and Omar simply stared, wide-eyed, as for a frozen moment everyone watched the awful scene in mounting horror.

Aunty recovered first.

'Aaaarghhhh!' she yelled, leaping from the chair faster than Jazeera believed was possible. Jogged by this sudden movement, Azra opened her mouth and . . . was sick again . . . and again. It sprayed in a wide crescent all over the beautiful ornaments, along the gleaming table-tops, and across the fabulous rugs. Azra's aim was impeccable. She missed nothing.

The next instant Jazeera's mother leapt up to catch Azra as Aunty released her into the middle of the stinking mess. She picked Azra up and ran for the nearest door out into the garden so that any more mess would not go on the furniture. But Azra had finished being sick. She sat blinking on the manicured lawn, looking decidedly pleased with herself, while her frantic mother searched for things to clean her up with.

Back in the house the quietly genteel atmosphere had been replaced by pandemonium. The new uncle jumped up, clapping his hands and repeatedly shouting for the servants who appeared with cloths and buckets.

The turbaned servant entered the room and began barking orders to the lesser servants as they scurried about sloshing water on to the floor. With great difficulty, Jazeera stifled a grin. The man's nose was thrust higher and higher into the air, to avoid the unpleasant smell beneath it.

Aunty had vanished, tight-lipped, into her room to wash and change while Jazeera's father apologised, in every other sentence, to his grim-faced cousin.

The uncle waved his hand dismissively.

'Don't worry about it,' he insisted firmly as he supervised the clearing-up operation.

Jazeera's father and Uncle Salim bent forwards to assist with the cleaning.

'I'm *so* sorry . . .'

'Here, let me . . .'

' . . . can't understand how it could have happened . . .'

'She's not usually . . .'

Uncle forced a smile on to his face. 'Don't worry. They will clean it.'

'But the water shortage . . .'

'Never mind. Never mind.'

Just then Aunty appeared in yet another stunning saree. This time though she looked flustered and uncomfortable. She gazed in disgust at the now watery mess. Uncle stood up and waved towards the door.

'Perhaps we should all go outside while they are cleaning.' It was more of a command than a suggestion and his smile only thinly disguised his true feelings.

As they followed the prim couple outside, Jazeera turned to Nani and giggled.

'I don't think that Aunty does like babies after all.'

5. The Snake Awakes

Dear Diary,

It is so hot now that my hands are all slippery. I can hardly hold my pen. This heat-wave is terrible, even Nani says that she can't remember it being as hot as this before. I have an awful headache, but at least I understand what the problem is. Poor Azra doesn't like the heat at all. She just cries and cries.

Mostly we stay indoors during the day with the doors and shutters closed to keep the rooms cool. We only go out in the evenings when it is not so hot.

Anil came round yesterday. He has written a reply to every single person in the class. I couldn't believe it! It must have taken him hours to write them all. He looked very pleased with himself.

Anil brought the Frisbee and threw it for Shebu a few times in the garden. She went wild with excitement trying to catch it. You would think that she would be too hot to run with all her fur in this terrible heat. But what a shock we had . . .

The Frisbee sliced through the hot air with colourful speed and landed on the far side of the garden, narrowly missing Aunty Naseema who was unpegging some clothes from the line. Shebu bounded after it with unrestrained delight.

'Maybe I should have bought one of these for Shebu,' laughed Jazeera. 'Mind you, I would have to teach Nani how to throw it, I can't see Aunty or Uncle having a go!'

Jazeera and Anil set off after the little dog but were stopped in their tracks by frantic barking. Shebu was behaving like a deranged lunatic in front of a large bush.

'What's the matter?' asked Anil.

His question was answered a moment later when a thin head flashed out of the bush and hissed warningly at Shebu.

Aunty, who was standing nearest the bush, dropped all the clothes that she was holding and shrieked at the top of her voice.

'SNAKE!'

Without pausing to recover, she tumbled headlong back towards the house, grabbing Jazeera and Anil on the way. Shebu followed close on their heels, having decided that the creature in the bush was none too friendly.

The entire household, except for Jazeera's father and Uncle Salim who were out, stood by the door, alerted by Aunty's screams. The minute the last person was in they slammed it shut and shot the heavy bolt across. Aunty promptly fainted in the arms of Jazeera's mother. A cup of cold water brought Aunty round and she lay trembling with fright on the sofa, aware of her narrow escape.

'What shall we do?' asked Jazeera's mother, conscious of the danger.

'I'll go and see if it is still there,' volunteered Nani. She went to the back bedroom and looked cautiously out of the window, but she couldn't see anything. The snake might have gone, but on the other hand, it might have retreated back into the bush.

'Someone left the gate open,' called

Omar from the front window. 'That's how it got in.'

Aunty moaned.

'We must telephone for help,' said Jazeera's mother, taking charge of the situation. She reached for the heavy black telephone but all she heard at the other end was a deafening silence.

'What's the matter with the phone?' she asked angrily.

'Oh no,' groaned Aunty. 'It's the twenty-fifth. The phone lines are down today for central repairs. They did announce it in the newspapers.'

'So then, we are trapped,' Nani said grimly.

Everyone looked at each other in silence.

'Only till Daddy gets back,' Omar piped up. 'Then he will go out and BASH it!' Omar swiped at the ground with an imaginary weapon. 'He will bash the snake on the head.'

'No,' said Nani. 'Your daddy and Uncle won't be back for a long time. I heard them saying that they would be late tonight.'

Azra chose that moment to announce that she was hungry. Jazeera's mother went to the fridge and let out a gasp. 'There's no milk left. I was going to go out and get some more. Azra drank it all at breakfast.'

Azra started to cry even louder.

'We have to do something,' said Jazeera's mother. 'Someone will have to go out.'

Aunty propped herself up on one elbow and pointed at Anil who crouched innocently in the corner of the room. 'You,' she called. 'You will have to go and get rid of that thing.'

'ME!' Anil croaked in disbelief.

'Well, we cannot stay trapped in the house with a screaming child all day. Go on.'

Anil stood up nervously. You could tell that he was just as scared of the snake as anyone else, but as a humble servant he daren't disobey the lady of the house.

'You can't send Anil,' shouted Jazeera.

'Be quiet, Jazeera,' snapped her aunt. Reaching behind the sofa she pulled out a heavy walking stick and thrust it into Anil's reluctant hands. 'Here, use this.'

Anil stood still. Aunty sank back on to the cushions. 'Jazeera, you hold the door open for the boy. But make sure that you close it quickly, we don't want that thing coming into the house.' She shivered violently at the thought.

Jazeera looked at the now quaking Anil. It wasn't fair to pick on him just because he was a servant. He needed help and none of the others were prepared to give any because they thought that he was inferior to them. So Jazeera hatched a plan.

Remembering her aunt's words, Jazeera closed the door quickly behind Anil . . . and herself. Ignoring the cries of protest coming from inside the house, she edged around the garden, followed by a startled Anil.

The two reached the corner of the house where the washing line began. In a direct line across the lawn was the bush, silent and unmoving. Was the snake still inside, watching their slow progress, ready to strike out? Jazeera gulped, her throat suddenly dry. She had been brave and determined inside the house, but now, out here in the silent garden, she began to wonder if she had done the right thing. Snake bites were supposed to be very painful if not deadly.

Pushing those thoughts to the back of

her mind, Jazeera gripped Anil's sweaty hand. They waited and watched. The bush did not move.

Jazeera's eye was caught by the bright yellow disc staring forgotten at the blue sky. They needed a distraction and that might just work. She whispered to Anil and pointed at the Frisbee. Anil tried to stop her, but it was no good. Jazeera tiptoed across the garden and gingerly picked up the hot plastic toy. She straightened up, her eyes fixed on the bush. The leaves rustled, and it wasn't the wind.

A sour taste poured into Jazeera's mouth. The taste of fear. Jazeera froze. She was sure that the thudding of her heart was loud enough to disturb a whole nest of vipers, but apart from the first rustle, the bush did not move. Gingerly she inched backwards until she felt the reassuring presence of Anil behind her.

Jazeera and Anil stood on the edge of the lawn clutching their weapons. From

the corner of her eye, Jazeera saw the worried figure of Nani at the bedroom window. She ignored it. Nothing must disturb her concentration now, or her aim. She mouthed the words silently at Anil:

'ONE . . .

TWO . . .

THREE.'

With deadly accuracy the Frisbee left Jazeera's clammy hands, swooped in a perfect arc and landed slap in the middle of the bush. In a trice the snake slithered out, shaken by the attack. It was then that Anil dashed forwards bashing the ground with his stick and uttering blood-curdling yells.

The onslaught was more than the snake could handle. With surprising speed it shot across the garden, hardly seeming to touch the ground. It veered around the gate and out into the comparative peace of the road, chased by a still screaming Anil who slammed the gate firmly shut. The last Anil saw of the snake, it was heading off into a deserted building site at the end of the street.

Jazeera joined Anil at the gate and threw her arms around him in joyful relief. 'You did it!' she cried.

Anil grinned. He had done it and he would never have believed it possible. Still he wouldn't have been able to do it on his own.

'You were great,' he said enthusiastically.

Nani, Aunty and Jazeera's mother ran down to the gate and hugged Jazeera, telling her what a brave, naughty, silly girl she had been. Jazeera looked up to see tears in her mother's eyes.

'What's wrong?' she asked.

'You might have been killed, Jazeera.'

'So might Anil.'

'But that's different.'

'Why?'

'It just is.'

'Well, you sent Anil off to fight the snake and he's not older than me, so if he could go then so could I.'

'That's not the point.'

Grown-ups can be infuriating at times.

Nani moved forward and put her arms around both Jazeera and Anil. 'You have both been very brave. I think that you should come inside and have a drink, and if I remember rightly, there might even be some ice cream left . . .'

Leaving the stunned women behind, Nani led the heroes back into the house for a suitable celebration.

Dear Diary,

It all came out today that Omar wants to buy himself a scooter. He has managed to save 500 rupees which works out at about £10. Omar was very upset when Uncle told him how much a scooter costs. Daddy sat Omar down and explained to him that, quite apart from the money, you have to be seventeen before you are allowed to ride on the roads.

Omar was furious after all the work that he had been doing to earn money. He thought that he could buy a scooter now and take it home with him to show all his friends at school. Little brothers can be really thick at times!

Anyway because he worked so hard Daddy said that they will open a savings account for him when we get home, to keep all his money safe. Daddy even said that if, by the time he is seventeen, Omar has saved up enough money to buy a motorbike then he will double it and buy Omar a car. Lucky so-and-so.

Perhaps I'd better start saving too.

6. Out in the Midday Sun

Saturday dawned clear and sunny. Another sweltering day. It was the Hindu festival of Rakshan Bandan and everybody took the day off.

'But we are Muslims,' said Jazeera.

'We celebrate everybody's festivals here,' laughed Uncle Salim. 'We are always enjoying ourselves.'

As Uncle's bangle shop was closed for the day he decided to take everyone for a picnic to the famous Minar Gardens.

In the scorching shade of the tall, crumbling Minar the family spread out their picnic. Aunty and Nani worked hard all morning preparing *samosas*, *naans*, *pakoras* and sweets. Jazeera glugged her refreshing drink thankfully and gazed up at the huge tower.

The site had been a mosque hundreds of years ago. Now all that was left of the massive building was the red stone tower covered with an intricate web of carvings, worn smooth with the winds of the years.

Nani stretched and stood up, eyeing the circling birds in the cloudless sky. 'Come on, girls, if you've finished we'll go for a walk.'

'Don't tire Nani out, will you, Jazeera?' called her mother. Jazeera and Ayisha grabbed a *samosa* each and followed Nani to the bottom of the ruin.

Nani told them about the king who had conquered the people of this area and ordered the mosque to be built. He had two sons and they both wanted to rule after him. One day, in the gardens of the mosque they had a fight. Both died. The king was so upset by his loss that he went into the mosque to pray and never came out again.

The king of a neighbouring area heard what had happened and sent in his army. With the king inside the mosque there was no one to lead the army and the soldiers fled from the invading forces. The neighbouring king ransacked the whole city and burnt the mosque down. All that remained was the Minar.

Jazeera and Ayisha listened intently, they loved it when Nani told them stories. They could almost see the anguished king praying in the magnificent tower. They could almost hear the clang of the swords as the city was terrorised. The acrid smell of burning almost reached their nostrils as Nani described the mosque blazing to the ground.

Huge black birds wheeled overhead. They landed on the blunt top of the massive tower. Buzzards, each bigger than Azra, surveyed the colourful gardens with tiny coal-black eyes.

The little group wandered over to a

bed of violet pink roses.

'What happened to the king, Nani?'

'No one ever found his body after the mosque was burnt. Some people say that he climbed to the very top of the tower and threw himself off into the flames.' The two girls stood and gazed at the enormous Minar towering above them.

'Some people say,' continued Nani softly, 'that the king can still be seen at the top of the tower weeping for his lost sons and ruined kingdom.'

Jazeera stopped chewing, her *samosa* poised halfway up to her mouth. Something moved on the top of the tower. She was sure that she saw a mysterious dark shape shifting. Curious, she shielded her eyes against the sun with her arm to look again. At an incredible speed, the shape lunged off the top of the tower and arrowed towards her. Jazeera screamed as it swooped over her head. It grabbed the remaining *samosa* in its talons. Wings

flapped furiously in her face. The force of the buzzard's wings hurled Jazeera to the ground and the bird of prey screeched away into the depths of the sky.

At once Nani and Ayisha were beside Jazeera pulling her up and checking that she was all right. Apart from a scratch on her hand Jazeera was unharmed, just shaken. Jazeera's parents, who had heard her scream, came rushing over and soon everyone was helping her back to the picnic area.

'That bird must have thought that you

were holding the food out for it,' said Ayisha wisely.

That bird,' said Aunty sagely, 'was a bad omen, if ever I saw one. You'd better be careful, Jazeera.'

'Well, I think that from now on I'll eat inside, Aunty. It's much too dangerous to eat outdoors in India.'

Dear Diary,

What a day we've had. Those buzzards gave me a real fright. I couldn't stop trembling even though Nani cuddled me for ages. I think that Ayisha got a bit fed up with me. Mind you, the worst bit was when it was time to go home. We clambered back into Uncle's old car and it was more uncomfortable than when we set off this morning. Anyway, to cut a long story short, the car wouldn't start.

Uncle got out and fiddled about inside the bonnet. Then Daddy went to help him. I don't think that Uncle appreciated the help from some of the words that I heard him say. We were all hot and irritable inside the car and Mummy was worried that Azra might be sick again!

After about an hour of trying, Uncle gave up. The car was broken and there was nothing else for it, we had to find some other way of getting home. Isn't it amazing that when you want a taxi, you can never find one? I was so hot and tired that at times I felt dizzy.

We all trudged into the town and eventually Daddy managed to get some rickshaw wallahs to take us to the railway station. We had to wait for another half an hour in a queue for our tickets. We only managed to get seats in third class and even then Daddy had to bribe the ticket man to let us have them. That bird really was a bad omen after all.

The carriages were crowded, dirty and incredibly noisy. The oily steam blew dust in their faces constantly and the

planks they were sitting on became harder and harder as the train chugged on.

At each station the swell of bodies shifted and shoved inside the cramped carriage. Chickens squawked and goats bleated as they were ushered on or off. Men squatted like sparrows on the flat-topped roof of each carriage, exposed to the glare of the sun and the constant blasts of smelly steam. At first Jazeera was worried about them falling off, but as the journey progressed she soon became preoccupied with her own discomfort.

Thankfully both Omar and Azra fell into fitful sleep almost as soon as the train started. Jazeera sat squashed between Nani and Ayisha. She closed her eyes and prayed for the journey to be over. Jazeera just wanted to get back to Nani's house, away from the sweaty smells of unwashed bodies and farm animals.

Jazeera's father sat grimly by the window taking the brunt of the grime from the steam. He was worried about Uncle Salim who had stayed behind with the car. Uncle would have to wait there until a mechanic arrived.

Nani groaned quietly and Jazeera's mother leant across the carriage and patted her arm.

'Are you all right?' she asked.

Nani nodded, holding her saree over her mouth in an attempt to stop some of the dust getting in. She closed her eyes against the mounting heat and congestion.

The journey was a living nightmare.

Everyone was tired and stressed but at long last the train rumbled into their station. The family prised themselves out of the train and into the jostling crowd on the platform.

Jazeera stretched her aching arms and legs; they had been in the same cramped position for so long she had lost all feeling in her toes. A large woman balancing an extremely large bundle of clothes on her head barged up to the train. Without waiting for everyone to get down she pushed past Nani, shoving her roughly aside as she clambered on board.

Nani fell against the side of the train, exhausted from the travelling. Aunty caught her and helped her to stand upright.

'Are you all right, Nani?' cried Jazeera in alarm.

Nani gave a weak smile. She teetered on her tired legs then collapsed with a soft cry on to the baking platform.

7. Nani in the Sun

The midday sun blazed its blanket of relentless heat over the garden. The doctor came out of Nani's room and whispered softly to Jazeera's mother on the verandah before pushing his sturdy bicycle down the drive and pedalling away.

Jazeera was desperate to go and see how her grandmother was. The doctor had been in with her for ages and Jazeera was worried. Her mother and Aunty bustled in first, telling the children sternly to stay where they were and not to make any noise.

Omar was busy filling in one of his colouring books and Azra played happily on the floor. For once, they were well behaved. It was as though, somehow, they understood the seriousness of the situation.

Jazeera stood outside Nani's door and screwed her eyes tightly shut.

'Please, God, make Nani better,' she prayed. 'I know that you can do it. You can do anything that you want to. We will be going home soon so please don't let her be ill for long.'

Just then the door to Nani's room swung open and the adults filed out.

'Nani wants to speak to you, Jazeera,' Aunty said gently.

'Now you must promise me that you will be a good girl. I know how boisterous you children can get and the doctor has said that Nani needs lots of rest.'

'I promise, Aunty.'

Jazeera entered the darkened room. The overhead fan whirled a cooling breeze over the bed, which stood in the centre of the room. Nani lay with her eyes closed enjoying the air circulating over her frail face. Her long grey hair swirled loose over the pillow, occasionally tugged this way and that by the breeze.

Jazeera tiptoed quietly over and sat on the hard wooden chair beside the bed. Nani looked as though she was asleep, so remembering what the doctor had said, Jazeera decided not to disturb her.

In the dim light, Jazeera watched the rise and fall of Nani's chest. Nani would be better after a nap. Whenever she had a headache Nani always had a nap. She said that they did her the world of good.

After a while, Jazeera leaned forward and took hold of the sleeping figure's hand. She hoped that perhaps some of her youth and strength would flow into the old lady and help her to recover. The hand felt dry and papery and Jazeera was surprised at how many bones she could feel. Nani must have lost a lot of weight in the two days since she collapsed at the train station. She would need fattening up as soon as she got better.

Jazeera was planning what food Nani might like to eat, when the old lady stirred and opened her eyes.

'Oh, I'm sorry, Nani,' said Jazeera. 'I wasn't supposed to wake you up.'

Nani's eyes were dull and watery but they fixed on Jazeera's face, and Nani smiled.

'I wanted to see you, Zeeraji,' she croaked.

'I'm here, Nani, don't worry, everything's going to be all right.'

Nani swallowed painfully and pointed at the glass of water on her bedside table. Jazeera helped Nani to sit up a little and held the glass to her lips. She was as light as a feather. Nani only took little sips but afterwards she seemed a little stronger.

'Come and sit here,' Nani said.

So Jazeera perched on the edge of the bed and held Nani's hand. Nani seemed to like that.

'Jazeera,' Nani said. 'There's something that I want to tell you. I want you
to know how happy you have made me.
I have been very fortunate in my life, I
had a good husband, two beautiful
children and three grandchildren. God
has certainly blessed me.'

Nani paused to take some deep
breaths.

'And you, Zeeraji,' she continued at
last, 'have been the jewel in my crown. I
hope and pray that one day you will be
lucky enough to be a Nani and have a

granddaughter like you. You have brought me so much joy.'

Jazeera blushed, she didn't know what to say.

'Jazeera darling, I will be going away soon,' Nani said softly.

'Where, Nani? Has the doctor said that you must have a holiday to recover?'

'No ... no ... I am not going on holiday. I am going to be with someone that I love very much.'

'Who's that, Nani?' Jazeera was puzzled.

'I have missed him for many years and since I have been ill I hear him calling to me in my sleep. It's your Nana. He is waiting for me and I am going to be with him again.'

'Nani, Nani, what do you mean?' A note of panic crept into Jazeera's voice as her numbed brain struggled to understand what Nani was trying to tell her. But Nani fell quiet and for a few moments just concentrated on getting her breath. When she had recovered Jazeera gave her another sip of water.

Nani opened her eyes and to Jazeera's surprise they glowed with a fierce brightness. The thin, cracked lips parted in a smile.

'I'm so happy, Zeeraji. You must believe me. I don't want you to be sad. Will you promise me that?'

Jazeera sat clutching the wafer-thin hand, not sure what to say.

'Promise me,' Nani urged.

Jazeera gulped, a lump rising in her throat.

'I promise,' she whispered.

Nani lay back, still smiling. The fierce look in her eyes was replaced by one of inner peace and contentment.

'Open the curtains please, Jazeera. I want to see the light outside.'

Jazeera got up and pulled back the finely woven material. A shaft of sunlight danced into the room and bathed Nani in its warmth. Nani closed her eyes against the sudden brightness.

Jazeera returned and sat beside the bed.

'I love you, Nani,' she said. But Nani couldn't hear her any more.

Dear Diary,

Nani died today. I was there. Everyone in the whole house is crying and lots of neighbours have come round, they are crying too.

For some reason I cannot cry. Nani told me not to be sad, but it's not just that. Nani wanted to die. She wanted to be with Nana. I know that I will miss her, but how can I be sad when she was so happy.

I will always love Nani and one day we will meet again. I'm certain of it. But today I'm just glad that she was so happy.

I'm glad that she died in the sun.

Words that you may not know:

Beyti	term of affection for a younger girl
Chaat	a savoury snack
Dhobi-wallah	laundryman
-ji	term of affection and respect
Minar	a tower
Naan	flat bread
Pakoras	deep fried snack
Rupees	Indian money
Samosas	spicy vegetables wrapped in pastry
Wallah	worker